The New Girl

by

Mary Hooper

First published in Great Britain by Barrington Stoke Ltd
10 Belford Terrace, Edinburgh EH4 3DQ
Copyright © 2003 Mary Hooper

The moral right of the author has been asserted in
accordance with the Copyright, Designs and
Patents Act 1988
ISBN 1-84299-101-9
Printed by Polestar AUP Aberdeen Ltd

A Note from the Author

If you're an only child (like Kirsty in this book, and like me) you'll know how important best friends are. And everyone knows that breaking up with your best friend can be just as awful as breaking up with your boyfriend.

Most of my books are about friendships, and this one is about a girl who is on the rebound from her best friend and so gets in just a little too deeply, too quickly, with a girl who wasn't all she seemed to be.

There's no moral to this book, but just remember this: best friendships can last forever, boyfriends usually don't!

Contents

Chapter 1

The Row

As we walked out of school, Bethan and I were arguing about where we were going to meet that evening. I suggested my house.

"Oh, that's just like you, Kirsty!" she said to me as we went through the school gates.

"What d'you mean?" I asked.

"You're just a selfish only child! We always have to meet where *you* want."

"We do not!" I said crossly. "What about the time I cycled three miles in the pouring rain to meet you in town?"

"That was only because I was going to buy you your birthday present!"

"It was not! You're a liar!" I shouted.

"No. *You're* a liar!" she said. "And what's more, you're a mean-faced, fat cow and no-one likes you!"

And as she said that, she ripped off the friendship bracelet I'd made her, threw it at me and stomped off.

I was stung by her words – did no-one like me? Really?

I was too upset to reply. I just stood there as she marched off down the road.

We had rows sometimes, we shouted and slagged each other off, but she'd never said anything so bitchy to me before. *How could she say something as mean as that? Was it true?*

"That was way out of order," I heard a voice behind me say, and I turned to see Carly standing there.

Carly was new to our school. She'd started halfway through the term and, to be quite honest, no-one had taken much notice of her. The rest of us had all been together for more than three years and had formed our little groups. She didn't seem to fit into any of them.

"Completely over the top," she said. "What a bitch. And she's supposed to be your best mate."

I nodded, still shocked.

"That was a horrible thing to say – and it's just not true. Anyone can see how popular you are."

I looked at her and smiled. "Well, I don't know about that. But I'd hate to think ... well, you know."

Carly shook her head. "She's a loser. Just ignore her. Freeze her out."

"Yeah, OK, I will."

A couple of older girls came past us giggling loudly about something, and we began to walk on.

Carly fell into step beside me. "You live down Meredith Road, don't you?"

I nodded. "What about you?"

"In York House. With Mrs Harding ... you've probably heard about her."

"Oh, yeah," I said, feeling a bit embarrassed because I hadn't remembered where she was living. York House was a foster home, and we often had girls from there coming to our school.

I guess that was another reason no-one had bothered to make friends with Carly – you never knew how long anyone from York House would be around. Sometimes they were staying there because they were going through a difficult time (that's how the teachers put it) and then went back to their parents after a while. Sometimes they'd run away from home, and sometimes their parents had kicked them out. They could be at school with us for two weeks, or for a year or more. Then they'd move on.

"Is it awful there?" I asked.

"Horrible," she said.

"Why are you ... I mean, why d'you have to live there?"

"My mum's new boyfriend. He used to beat me up. And worse," she said.

"*Really?*" I stared at her. "Didn't your mum try and stop him?"

Carly shook her head. "My mum never liked me. She used to starve me when I was little. She got rid of my two sisters – had them adopted."

I was shocked. I would have liked to have asked more but I didn't want to upset her. Instead, we started chatting about boys and stuff, and bands we liked, and clothes, and she said she loved the way I did my hair.

"It's dead easy to do," I said, because I always wore it the same way, in a bun on the top of my head, with a little, spiky fringe. "When I get up in the morning I just swish it up, stick a scrunchy round it and it's done."

"It suits you," Carly said. "Looks very cool. You *are* cool, you know."

"You're kidding!" I laughed.

"I'm not. Even school uniform looks all right on you."

"Now I know you're having me on!"

We both started laughing. Then I realised that I'd gone from being really upset about what Bethan had said, to hardly bothering about it at all.

Carly and I carried on chatting and got on so well that by the time we'd reached my house, we'd arranged that she'd come and call for me the next morning. That way, we'd be together when we passed Bethan's house and I wouldn't have to feel embarrassed.

I went indoors quite pleased with myself. I'd fallen out with my best friend – but it looked like I already had a replacement.

Chapter 2
The Silver Chain

"What lovely manners!" Mum said to me a few days later. "Your friend Carly's very polite, isn't she – especially considering she's living in a foster home."

"Ssshh!" I said, frowning towards the sitting room where I'd left Carly chatting to Dad. "She'll hear you."

"Well, you have to give it to her, Kirsty," Mum said to me as she put the kettle on for tea. "You don't expect girls like that – girls from foster homes – to have such nice manners. That was a lovely bunch of roses she gave me. None of your friends has ever brought me flowers before."

I rolled my eyes.

Then Mum changed the subject. "What about Bethan?" she asked.

"What about her?"

"You haven't made up with her, then?"

I shook my head, then got some biscuits out of a tin and arranged them on a plate. "She tried to talk to me in Art today but I just turned my back on her."

"Kirsty! That wasn't very nice."

"What she said to me wasn't very nice," I said. "And anyway, I've got Carly now."

When we went back to the sitting room, Dad was grinning at something Carly had said, all pleased with himself. "What d'you know, Kirsty," he said. "Your friend reckons I look like George Clooney!"

Mum and I burst out laughing.

"He does!" Carly said. "He's got the same smile ... and the crinkly eyes."

"Crinkly eyes! Oh, he's got those all right," Mum said.

"But I didn't realise George Clooney had such a beer gut!" I added, poking Dad in the stomach.

I told Carly to grab some biscuits. "Come on – we'll go up to my room and listen to a CD."

Carly hesitated. "Is that all right with you?" she asked Mum.

"Course it is, love," Mum said. "You two go off and make as much noise as you like."

"Thank you very much for the meal," Carly said to her. "It was really lovely."

"It was only pizza!" said Mum, but she was grinning.

"Homemade, though," Carly said. "I don't think I've ever had homemade pizza before. It was so much tastier than the bought ones."

"Well, you must come round for a proper meal soon," Mum said.

"*Si, si,*" Dad said in his fake Italian accent. "I will do you my spaghetti with garlic and seafood."

Carly laughed. "Can't wait!" she said.

"Come on!" I said to her, pushing her out of the sitting room. "He'll be taking you step by step through how he makes it if you're not careful."

She followed me upstairs to my room. "Your mum and dad are so nice," she said, sitting down on my bed. "You're really lucky, you know."

I shrugged.

"No, really you are. Not many girls have mums and dads who'd bother to even *speak* to someone from a foster home. Lots of people think we're bad, see. Damaged goods. Sale or return." She looked around my bedroom. "This is a cool room," she said.

I pulled a face. "It's just ordinary."

"It's not! I reckon it's really special – these purple walls and white cupboards – and

I love those bare floorboards and that fluffy rug."

"What's yours like, then?"

She made a sick noise. "Flowery wallpaper and curry-coloured carpet."

"Really?"

"And it's not just mine. I have to share it with a girl called Chelsea, and I don't know how long I'm going to be there, so it's hardly worth doing anything to it."

"What's Chelsea like, then?" I asked.

Carly screwed up her nose. "She's a cow. She's two years older than me and she treats me like I'm her slave or something. She expects me to clean her shoes!"

"Really? Can't you complain to Mrs Harding? Ask to be moved or something?"

She made a sound of disgust. "She doesn't give a damn! Anyway, if I tried to say anything, Chelsea would beat me up."

"No way," I said. It all sounded awful. I couldn't bear to live like that.

Carly suddenly sprang to her feet. "Can I look at your clothes?" she said. "I bet you've got some class stuff. You always look so cool whatever you're doing."

She flung open my wardrobe doors. "Wow! Such a lot of gear. Where do you go to wear it all?"

I shrugged. "Well, I've got this boyfriend who's a couple of years older than me – Tim. I hang out with him and his mates sometimes. And there's a club in town we go to when we've got any money."

"Tim. Is he gorgeous? Is he really special?"

I smiled. "He's all right."

"Bet he is! You wouldn't go out with someone ordinary. Who does he look like on TV that I'd know?"

I thought about this, and then I got out my box of bits and pieces and found a photo of Tim and we discussed whether or not he looked like the new guy in *EastEnders*. In the box I also found a photo of the two of us together which had been taken on Tim's birthday. Carly said we made a brilliant couple and really looked like an item.

She flopped back on my bed, holding the photo, just staring at it. "One day I want to be like you and have someone like Tim," she sighed. "One day I want to get adopted by a proper family in a real house and have a lovely room and a boyfriend and everything like you've got."

Some chance, I thought, but I couldn't say that.

"Well, I expect you will!" I said.

"And when I've got all that," Carly went on, "if there's anyone around who's living in a foster home I'm going to be really, really friendly to them. Like your family are to me."

"Oh, forget it!" I said. I was feeling guilty about my life sounding so good while hers was rubbish. I wanted to change the subject. "Which CD do you want?" I asked, and we lay back on the bed to listen.

****

Later, when she'd gone home, I put my photos back and took a moment to look through the other stuff in the box. It was then that I realised that a really pretty silver chain was missing. Tim had given it to me. I'd put it in the box last week because I'd broken it – I was going to take it into town and have it repaired.

I took everything out of the box, searching for the chain. Then I realised that, because it was so thin, it had probably slipped out and fallen between two floorboards. I decided I wouldn't tell Tim, in case he thought I hadn't been looking after it properly. Maybe I could buy another one just like it and he'd never know.

I didn't want to upset him because, like Carly had said, he *was* special.

I thought about Carly. Yes, I was lucky all right. Lucky not to have a life like hers.

Chapter 3

The Boyfriend

"Carly's a real mate," I said to Tim. It was a week or so later and we were on our way to meet her.

Tim had been given three free tickets to a special showing of the new James Bond film at the local cinema, and I'd asked him if she could come as well.

I'd thought it would be nice for them to get to know each other, and maybe if she was around a while longer, he'd be able to fix her up for a date with one of his mates.

"I feel sorry for Carly," I told him. "She's had an awful life. Her stepfather beat her up – or worse – and her mum didn't want her."

Tim shrugged. "It happens." He had a stepfather himself. He didn't get beaten up or anything, but they fought a lot and his stepfather had once told Tim he'd throw him out if he didn't behave.

"And she has two sisters, but she's lost touch with them because her mum had them both adopted," I went on.

"Sounds bad."

"So you will be nice to her, won't you?"

"Course I will," he grinned, "especially if she's a bit of a babe."

I gave him a push and we walked on, laughing.

Carly was waiting for us at the bus station. She greeted us happily and I saw, to my surprise, that she was wearing her hair up in a bun. Just like mine. What was more, she had a little, spiky fringe, too. I thought that was a bit odd.

"You must be Tim," she said, smiling up at him. "I've heard all about you!"

Tim grinned. "Good things, I hope."

She gave him a look from under her long, black eyelashes. "*Very* good things," she said in a low, sexy voice.

I was really embarrassed when she said it like that. And Tim was, too. He didn't know what to say.

Carly didn't seem to notice, though, she just started talking about TV and filmstars and saying she adored Brad Pitt and what she'd do for him she wouldn't like to say. Stuff like that.

In the cinema Tim sat between us, and I noticed Carly leaning towards him, closer and closer as the film went on. Once, when there was a scary bit, she shrieked and buried her head in his jacket.

At first I'd thought that we'd all go for a coffee on the way home, but in the end I just didn't feel like it. Not after seeing the way Carly was all over Tim. I told her I ought to get back and finish my homework.

"Oh!" she wailed. "Really? I thought we were going on somewhere after the film."

"No, I'd better get back. We'll leave you at the bus station, OK?" I said.

She pouted at Tim. "If you must ..." she said, giving him a look and fluttering her eyelashes.

We left her at the bus station. As we walked off down the road, Tim gave a big sigh of relief. "Phew! What's *she* on?" he said. "What a freak."

"I know," I said. "Sorry. I didn't realise she'd be like that."

"She's like a cat on heat," he said. "She was all over me in the cinema – leaning on me and trying to play footsie with me."

I shook my head, puzzled. "I can't understand it," I said. "I'm really sorry."

"Must be something to do with not having any family," Tim said.

****

When Carly came to call for me the next morning, I had a real go at her. "You were so embarrassing!" I said. "Do you always carry on like that with your mates' boyfriends?"

She looked at me, confused. "I was just being friendly ..."

"Friendly!" I exploded. "If that's friendly, I'd hate to see you when you fancy someone."

"Well, maybe I was flirting a bit with him, but ..."

"It was more than that. You were *throwing* yourself at him!" I said. "You were trying to get off with him."

She stopped walking and stared at me, her bottom lip trembling. "Oh, Kirsty, I'm sorry," she said. "I just didn't think. I suppose it did look ... I mean, I thought you had to be like that with boys. I thought if I behaved like that, he'd like me. And I just wanted him to like me."

"But how did you think *I'd* feel?"

She shook her head. "I didn't think about it. I know I flirt a lot with boys. I try not to, but I can't seem to behave any other way."

"Well, you're going to have to try a bit harder," I said shortly. I started to walk on but she was still standing there, looking miserable. "Come on!" I called back. "We're going to be late."

"Kirsty," she said, running to catch me up, "you do still like me, don't you?   You won't stop hanging round with me?"

"No, of course not," I said crossly.

"Because if I thought I'd lose you as a friend ..." Her voice was sounding choked. "You're the best friend I've ever had. I don't want to lose you."

I sighed, but gave her a matey sort of slap on the shoulders. "Don't be daft."

"Will you help me?" she asked eagerly. "You know how to do things. Will you show me how to be normal with boys?"

"If you like," I said.

"That's all I want. To be normal," she said sadly.

I walked on. I didn't say another word. I'd just seen something, you see, and it had thrown me a bit. Through her white school shirt I'd caught a glimpse of a silver chain, and it had looked a lot like the one I'd lost.

I tried to get rid of the thought. A silver chain was a silver chain – they all looked pretty much alike.

Of course it wasn't mine.

Chapter 4

The Job

About a week later I saw a notice in the window of our newsagents. STUDENT WANTED TO HELP OUT AT VET'S SURGERY, it said, and it was just what I'd been looking for. It was the sort of casual job I could do in the evenings and possibly in the school holidays.

Apart from the fact that I loved animals, I also wanted the cash. There were loads of things I wanted to buy – and one of them was something special to wear to Mel's birthday party.

Mel was in our class and her dad was renting out the top floor of a club in town called The Cavern in two weeks' time. Loads of kids from school were going. We were all really looking forward to it.

I got Mum to ring the vet's surgery and tell them that I was dead keen to have the job and that I'd be in at the weekend to see them. I told Carly about it, of course, but I didn't tell anyone else at school in case they got in there before me.

Carly and I were still getting on great, so I hadn't said anything to her about the chain I'd seen her wearing. She hadn't worn it since, and I'd decided that it couldn't possibly be mine. Loads of people had silver chains.

At school, Bethan had tried to make friends with me a couple of times, but I'd just been polite to her, coolly polite, and turned away. I really didn't need someone like her, someone that put me down, now that I had Carly.

Carly, you see, thought I was the best. I suppose that was why she copied me all the time. I should have been flattered, but in fact I found it quite annoying. Carly not only had my hairstyle, she'd also started using the same pale, shimmery lipstick that I liked and had made some wire earrings with beads just like mine.

She had also started to wear my favourite perfume. When I jokingly pointed these things out to her, she did say she was sorry.

"But I like everything you wear and everything you do," she said to me once.

How do you reply to that?

On Saturday morning I got up early instead of lying in bed half the day like I usually do, and put on what Mum calls 'smart clothes'. She'd said that although I'd probably only be emptying trays of cat litter, I should wear something decent for the interview.

Hoping that they might ask me to start work straight away, though, I took an old T-shirt and jeans along in a bag.

I was quite excited about going there – and a bit jittery, too. Mum had told them that I'd be there at eleven o'clock and I was dead on time.

I pushed open the door of the surgery. I queued up behind a woman holding a

Pekingese dog under each arm, and told the girl behind the counter that my mum had already rung and I'd come about the job.

She looked at me, surprised. "I'm sorry," she said, "but it's already gone."

I was stunned. "But ... my mum phoned. She said I'd be in today."

The girl shook her head. "Sorry. It was first come, first served," she said. "A girl came in on Wednesday and she seemed all right, so we ..."

I didn't hear the rest, because my eyes had travelled past her to the back of the surgery, where the sick animals were kept.

Standing there, replacing a water feeder in the rabbit's cage, was Carly. Carly in a white overall with a namebadge on, looking as if she'd been there all her life.

I think I must have made a noise, a gasp of surprise, because Carly suddenly looked across and saw me. We stared at each other for a long moment and then I just turned and ran out.

I was furious for the rest of the day. Furious and a bit tearful. How *could* she? I'd told her about the job on Wednesday, so she must have gone straight round the minute we'd left each other.

She'd *known* how much I wanted it.

Mum said I shouldn't get too upset about it. She said that there would be plenty of other jobs and that I should have gone there myself at once if it had been *that* important.

I wondered what would happen the following Monday. Would Carly still come round for me in the morning? If she didn't, should I have a real go at her in front of everyone at school, or just ignore her?

In the event I didn't have to do either of these because she came around at six o'clock that same evening. If I'd known it was her at the door, I wouldn't have answered it, but I did, and of course, by then it was too late.

"Kirsty, please!" she said, putting her foot on the mat so I couldn't shut the door on her. "I just want to explain."

"There's nothing to say," I said stiffly. "You went behind my back and took my job. You knew how much I wanted it!"

"I did – and I'm really sorry," she said. "I just had to have a job, though. Look, let me tell you ..."

"I'm not interested," I said. "Just go!"

When I said that she burst into tears, and then Mum came through from the kitchen and saw her, and told me to invite Carly in and not have a row on the doorstep where all the neighbours could see us.

Carly was in the house in a flash. She followed me upstairs and I just sat on the bed silently while she told me everything.

From what Carly said, she owed Mrs Harding a lot of money. She'd borrowed money from her for make-up and perfume (*yes, I thought, and I know which brands*). She'd also taken some money from a petty cash float that they kept at the house.

She said that Mrs Harding was asking for the money back that she'd lent her, and if she found out that Carly had borrowed from the petty cash as well, then she'd be in serious

trouble. "They might have me up in court!"
she said to me, tearfully. "So, you see, I had
to get that job and replace what I owed."

Well, when she told me all that, and about
how she'd just wanted to buy things to be the
same as me and the other girls, I began to
feel sorry for her. And of course I wouldn't
have wanted to see her locked up.

So I ended up forgiving her, and she
stayed on to have an Indian takeaway with us.

It turned out to be quite a good evening,
in fact. She asked Dad all about when he was
a teenager and he told her some horror stories
about what he'd got up to when he was young.

Mum and I had heard them all before, of
course, but Carly was loving it and hung on to
every word. Mum said to Dad later, laughing,
that Carly had been flirting with him and he'd
been enjoying it.

I was just glad everything was cleared up
and we were friends again.

Chapter 5

The Misunderstanding

Carly started working at the vet's two or three evenings a week, so I didn't see quite so much of her as before. The following Friday, though, I had to stay late for drama club at school – they were giving out the parts for the end of term show. When I got home Carly had got there before me and was sitting in the kitchen with Mum.

As I went in, they were laughing about something, and then they stopped suddenly.

"Talk of the devil!" Mum said, still chuckling.

I frowned. I wasn't in the best of moods because I hadn't been given a part in the play. "What were you talking about, then?"

"Oh, just about how you spend hours in the bathroom dabbing lotion on a spot that no-one else can see."

Carly started giggling.

"Is that so funny?" I asked, a bit moodily. I sat down. "Don't I get made a cup of tea, then?" I asked, nodding towards Carly's mug.

"Kirsty! Don't be such a grouch," said Mum.

"I'll get you one," Carly said, getting up. She knew where the teabags and everything else were. Quite at home, she was.

Mum had another cup, too, and then asked Carly if she wanted to stay for supper that evening as she'd made a chilli and there was loads of it.

Asking her to eat with us again! I thought. I frowned at Mum slightly, to put her off, but she didn't seem to notice.

"I'm seeing Tim later," I said. Meaning, what was Carly going to do when I went out?

"That doesn't matter!" Mum said. "Carly can spend the evening with us. I'm sure even sitting in front of the telly with us oldies is better than an evening at the Home."

"Oh, it is!" Carly said. "And that'd be really nice, if you're sure it isn't too much trouble."

"Of course it's not, love," Mum said. Carly gave her a beaming smile and then looked at me, rather pleased with herself.

When Carly went upstairs to the loo a bit later, I said something to Mum about her being here again, and how it was beginning to seem as if she belonged in the house more than I did.

"Don't be so silly," Mum said. "The trouble with you, Kirsty, is that you're an only child, and only children do tend to become rather selfish. You're just not used to sharing."

I looked at her, a bit stung. She was saying just what Bethan had said.

"And we were only teasing you earlier. You should be used to a joke by now!"

I didn't say anything more. Maybe I was making a fuss about nothing.

****

I went out to meet Tim at about eight o'clock. I knew Carly wanted to come with me because she kept banging on about how gorgeous he was and how she'd like to see him again. But I didn't take any notice.

In fact, Tim was a bit odd with me when I saw him, and it wasn't until the end of the evening that I found out why. He said that he'd spoken to Carly at school and she'd told him that I might not be coming out that evening because I had 'something else on'.

"*What?*" I said, amazed.

"That's exactly what she said to me – that you had something else on," he repeated. "I thought from the way she spoke that you

41

were going out with someone else. I half expected you not to turn up tonight."

I gasped. "You're joking!"

He shrugged. "Well, maybe I read too much into it. It was just the way she said it, though."

I shook my head slowly. "She's got some explaining to do."

****

Carly was still at home when I got back. When I went into the sitting room she jumped up, thanked Mum and Dad for having her, and said she ought to be getting off.

She was about to disappear out of the front door when I stopped her. "Hang on, Carly," I said. "What did you say to Tim when you saw him today?"

"I haven't seen Tim! What d'you mean?"

"You haven't seen him?"

Her eyes opened, big and innocent. "No, of course not!"

"Didn't you bump into him at school?"

"Oh – that! I thought you meant seeing him properly – going out with him or something." She laughed, "I just spoke to him for a second or two. I've hardly *seen* him."

"But what did you say?"

"Nothing! Oh, I remember – just that you'd be staying at school late. For drama club."

I blinked at her. "Is that all?"

"Yes, of course. What am I supposed to have said?"

"Well, somehow he got the idea that I wasn't going to turn up tonight. That I was seeing someone else."

"*What?*" Now it was her turn to look amazed. "I just said you'd be at school until late."

"Are you sure that was all?"

"Of course!"

"OK," I said slowly. It was my mistake, then.

Chapter 6

The Very Short Skirt

A week or so later, Tim and I were waiting for Carly outside the ice skating rink.

I wasn't that keen, but Carly had insisted on treating Tim and me to a night out to make up for the meals she'd had at my house. I'd said that it wasn't necessary, and asked her if she'd paid back the money she'd borrowed from Mrs Harding, but she'd said she didn't want to talk about that.

When she came along the road towards us, my heart sank. From the waist up she looked just like me. She was wearing a blue rugby shirt (she'd bought one identical to mine), had her hair up, wore bead earrings and a pale, shimmery lipstick.

But I was wearing old jeans, and she had a short skirt. A *very* short skirt. "Have you got jeans with you?" I asked her.

She shook her head. "Why?"

I just looked at her.

"Because you're going to get a cold bum!" Tim said. "Unless you can skate really well."

She shrugged. "I've never been before. And I didn't think about wearing jeans. Why would I? When you see skaters on telly they always have short skirts."

"But they don't fall down," I said.

We went in and she insisted on paying, and then we hired boots and eased our way onto the ice.

I'd been three or four times before, but I could rollerblade so at least I knew how to stay up, and Tim was quite good anyway.

Carly, though, was rubbish. She couldn't stand up on her own, so wanted Tim to take her around. And when he did, she clung onto him the whole time, shrieking. When she wasn't clinging she was falling over, giggling madly and showing Tim and the rest of the rink her knickers.

The annoying thing was, Tim didn't seem to mind about how dippy she was. He did his best to show her how to balance and make her way round, and never lost it with her.

When I tried the same thing, though, hanging onto him in a really girlie way and asking him to take me round, he just laughed and said I was perfectly able to look after myself.

I tried to catch Tim's eye a couple of times, then glance at Carly and roll my eyes up in despair, but he didn't seem to realise what I was getting at.

It was a horrible evening and as far as I was concerned it couldn't be over fast enough. "I thought you found her embarrassing," I said to Tim as soon as we'd left Carly that night. "I thought you didn't like her."

He shrugged. "I don't like her. Not much."

"Well, how come you were all over her, then?"

"I was just trying to help."

"*Help?*" I spluttered.

"That's all it was! She doesn't have any idea about skating and I thought I'd help her.

I thought that's what you wanted – for me to be nice to her," Tim said.

"Well, I do," I said. "Sort of. But not *that* nice. You were all over her and I felt left out."

"Don't be so daft," he said. "I'm not interested in her. I'm going out with you, aren't I?"

"Are you *sure* you're not interested in her?"

"Sure," he said. He pulled me into his arms.

I pulled back. "She's got nice legs, though, hasn't she? And you saw enough of them tonight."

"They're all right. So are yours, though." He looked at me, head on one side. "Now I come to think of it, she looks a bit like you."

"She does *now*!" I said. "She's copied my hairstyle and my make-up and everything."

He began to laugh. "Ease up, Kirsty!" he said. "You're getting paranoid. The girl is new and she hasn't got any family or friends so she's attached herself to you, that's all. Don't be so selfish."

I stared at him. That word again – *selfish*. First Bethan had called me it, then Mum and now Tim.

I sighed. "Sorry," I said. "It's just that ... I don't want to lose you."

"Yeah, well, if there's any danger of Britney Spears coming after me, I'll let you know. Until then ..." He put his arms around me again and this time I didn't pull away.

I wanted things to be right. I wasn't going to let Carly come between us.

Chapter 7
The Right Gear

"What are you wearing to Mel's party?" I asked Carly on our way to school a few days later.

"Not sure," she said. "I'll probably buy something new. Might surprise you!"

Well, you've got the money seeing as you've got my job, I felt like saying.

She linked her arm with mine. "What are *you* wearing?"

"Dunno yet," I said, a bit fed up.

The party was on Friday and I had no hope of buying anything new before then.

I was trying to decide between two tops that I'd already worn before. One was a black cropped top with silver-sequinned straps which was a bit Abba but fairly OK. The other was an electric blue stretchy top which clung like a second skin. My tight, black trousers would go with either of them and it was just a matter of deciding which one I felt better in.

I tried on both outfits at home that night and went down to show Mum. She wasn't much help, though – she said they both looked a bit tarty and what was wrong with a nice, white shirt?

Sighing, I went upstairs again to study myself in my bedroom mirror. The trouble was, I'd worn each of them a few times already and I was tired of them.

I wanted to wear something exciting and new.

I took off the black top and, as I wasn't seeing Tim that night, changed into my old tracksuit and started doing a bit of homework.

At about nine o'clock there was a knock at the door and Mum called out that it was Carly. Before I could pretend I was in the bath or something she charged up the stairs and into my bedroom, looking really excited.

"Guess what?" she said. "I've just heard that my mum's coming to take me out tomorrow night!"

"Really?" I asked, not knowing if this was good news or not.

She nodded. "I'm so excited! I reckon she might ask me to go back and live with her."

"But d'you want to?" I asked. "I thought she was horrible to you. And what about her boyfriend?"

"She might have kicked him out!" Carly said, her eyes gleaming. "She never sticks with them for long."

"That's good, then," I said. "But then ... I suppose that means you'll be leaving our school."

"Dunno yet," she said. "I'd better not get too high about it." Her eyes drifted round the room, looking at the clothes scattered everywhere. "But I've come to ask you a favour."

"What's that, then?"

"I want something special to wear tomorrow night. I want to look really nice so my mum can see I'm looking after myself."

"Well, can't you wear whatever you're going to wear to Mel's birthday party?" I asked.

"I haven't bought it yet!" she said. "I was going out in my lunchtime on Saturday."

She suddenly saw the black top with silver-sequinned straps and pounced on it. "Oh, Kirsty, could I possibly borrow this?"

I hesitated. "Well, no, not really," I said. "I was thinking of wearing it to Mel's. It was either that or my blue one."

"Oh, please!" she said. "It'll mean so much to me to look good for my mum. And that blue top looks mint on you. It really shows off your figure."

"I don't know ..."

"Or you could still wear the black anyway. I'll only have it on a couple of hours and I'll really look after it. Oh, please, Kirsty! Just think, you might be helping to get me and my mum back together again. I might not have to stay at that awful York House any longer. I might be able to go home to my mum!"

Well, what could I say? I didn't want to be accused of being selfish again, so I lent it to her. I made her promise to take care of it, and not get food down it, and to give it back to me without fail on Thursday morning so I'd have time to decide if I was going to wear it to Mel's or not. And off she went with it.

Carly talked about the coming meeting with her mum all the following day and went home dead excited.

On Thursday morning she came round for me as usual. "So how did it go?" I asked straight away.

She just started crying. "She didn't turn up!" she said. "I waited and waited and she didn't come."

"But why not?" I asked. "Did she send any sort of message?"

"She rang later on and said something else had cropped up and that she'd be in touch soon."

I got my schoolbag and we began to walk along the street. Carly was still crying noisily, and every so often I patted her shoulder and made what I hoped were comforting remarks. I couldn't imagine what it must be like to be stood up by your mum.

"There's worse!" she said suddenly, turning to me. "I didn't know how to tell you before, but something awful's happened to your top!"

I'd actually been wondering where it was and whether she'd brought it with her, but hadn't liked to ask. Now my heart sank. "*What's* happened to it?"

"Well, Mrs Harding had just been to tell me that Mum wasn't coming after all, and I was so upset that I just ran into my bedroom, pulled my clothes off and got into bed. The thing was, I heard something tear and when I looked this morning, your top had split right down one side. The seam had ripped."

She gave me a pleading look. "You won't be cross with me, will you? I'll get you another one. I promise I will!"

I didn't know what to say. How could I have a go at her when she was so upset already?

"I don't think you'll be able to get another one," I muttered. "I bought it in London last year. Can't it be mended?"

"No, it's past all that," she said. "But look, I'll buy you something better. Something fabulous that you can wear on Saturday. You just wait!"

Chapter 8

The Sting

But the fabulous something didn't arrive. Carly didn't even mention it – even though I dropped hints. So on Saturday evening, I got ready for the party and put on my blue top. This, I had decided in the meantime, looked awful.

I'd agreed with Tim earlier that he'd go to the party with his mates and I'd go with Carly. But when she phoned on Saturday and said that she had to work late and couldn't make it round to mine on time, I wasn't surprised. She was always changing arrangements or getting into a muddle about times.

I'd begun to feel more than a bit uneasy about her, actually. There were things about her that just didn't hang together. I wasn't sure I believed all the stories she told me. Some of them changed slightly each time she told them – like she now had *three* sisters who'd been adopted, and her mum's boyfriend was called Martin, whereas earlier he'd been called Bill. I didn't even know if she'd really been going out with her mum on Wednesday.

However, I agreed to meet her at eight o'clock in the town square, which was right near The Cavern.

"I'll get the bus in. You *will* wait for me, won't you?" she'd pleaded. "I wouldn't dare walk around on my own in a place like that."

"Course I'll wait for you," I said. "Just don't be late." I'd decided I was going to say something to her that evening about my top. And I'd also say something about some books she'd borrowed, and a CD which she seemed to have forgotten about.

I made myself look as good as I could in the awful blue top. I put on my make-up with extra care and rubbed a bit of glitter moisturiser onto my arms like you do for a party. Dad dropped me off in the square just before eight o'clock.

8.15 p.m. came and went. I saw a few people I knew on their way to the party and I shouted to them that I'd be along soon.

Then it was 8.30 p.m. I fumed and paced around, getting crosser and crosser. Parties in clubs were few and far between and I was missing a great time!

I decided I'd wait until the next bus was due in and if she hadn't arrived by then I'd leave her to it. She knew where The Cavern was. She'd just have to brave it on her own.

It was 8.45 p.m. when I decided I wasn't going to wait any longer.

I walked along to the club and was told to go up the little, winding staircase where Mel's party was.

At the top, the first person I saw was Bethan, standing with a friend of Tim's. I was set to walk past her into the main room where they were dancing, but she gasped when she saw me and pulled me to one side. "Look," she said, "I maybe shouldn't say anything, but if you're looking for Tim, he's in the chill-out room with Carly."

I stared at her, horrified. "That's an awful thing to say!" I said. "Carly's not even here!" And I turned my back on her and pushed my way into the party room.

It was hot and crowded and noisy as I forced myself through everyone and made my way to the bar, looking for Mel. When I found her I gave her my present and wished her happy birthday and all that, then got a drink and just stood for a moment in the middle of all the party noise and bustle, wondering what to do.

I couldn't help thinking about what Bethan had said. Why would she say something like that? Because she was still trying to get back at me?

Or because it was true?

Could it *possibly* be true?

Once I'd let that thought in, I knew I had to go to the chill-out room. I asked where it was and was told to look for a red, velvet-covered door. Beyond it was a large room hung with dark tapestries. It was full of soft sofas and chairs. A chant CD was playing and it was candle-lit, really cool – and so dark that I stumbled over something and had to stand still for a moment until my eyes got used to the darkness.

Then I saw Tim – I recognised the bright green shirt I'd bought him for Christmas. He was standing against the far wall. He had his arms around a girl whose face I couldn't see, and he was kissing her.

I was so shocked that I couldn't move for a moment. How *could* he?

Then rage took over. I took three steps across the room and tapped him sharply on the shoulder. He wheeled round and I saw that it was Carly he was kissing.

Carly wearing my black top with the silver-sequinned straps.

Carly with my hair, make-up, perfume and earrings. *And* she was wearing my silver chain.

There was a strange, unreal moment when the three of us just stared at each other.

Tim looked at me and then at Carly. Then he said to me in a horrified voice, "Kirsty! I don't believe it. I thought that Carly was you!"

Carly and I looked at each other and it felt so weird. Like finding you've got a twin.

She smiled sweetly at us both. "So! I can do it as well as her, can't I, Tim? What d'you think? I'm just as good at kissing, aren't I?"

"Get out, you bitch!" I said. "Get out *right now* before I have you thrown out."

I was shaking with anger.

"Don't worry, I'm going." She looked Tim up and down. "You're not bad," she said, "but not fantastic. Score six out of ten."

I wanted to scream and yell and shake her. But I was so amazed and shocked that I didn't do any of those things.

Carly just smiled at us again and went out.

Tim shook his head in amazement.
"I just ... just don't believe it," he said in a shocked voice. "She looked like you, spoke

like you – even *smelt* like you. And in this dim light ..."

"It's OK," I said. I took his hand. "We've both been taken in by her. It's not your fault." I shook my head, "She's just been playing with us. She set me up. She's a lot cleverer than we thought."

The door opened again, letting in a burst of hot air and music, and Bethan appeared, peering round for us.

"Carly's just left the club," she said. "She was grinning all over her face."

I nodded.

Bethan looked at me. "I tried to tell you. I overheard her giving a message to someone to tell Tim that Kirsty would meet him in the chill-out room."

"I never said any such thing!" I said.

"I know!" Bethan said. "And I knew something dodgy was going on because – well, her hair and everything. She looked just like you. She was your double."

"She even had my top on," I said.

Bethany nodded. "I recognised it. You bought it when we went to London together last year."

"So we did." I gave her an apologetic smile. "Last year when we were mates."

We grinned at each other and I knew that we would be mates again. And as for Carly – well, that girl had problems. Real problems. Luckily, it wouldn't be me who had to sort her out.

Barrington Stoke would like to thank all its readers for commenting on the manuscript before publication and in particular:

Carl Claricoates
Rachel Cripps
Rachel Gray
Mrs C. Hodgson
Aaron Humphrey
Zakiya N. Hussein
Sam Jeffrey
Lisa Love
Daniel Maddocks
Peter Martin
Sophie McEwan
Carol McMain
Daniel Mitchell
Niamh Munday
Margaret Pimm
Georgina Pole
Ben Rodgers
Daniel Sparkes
George Stewart
Kirsty Wright

Become a Consultant!

Would you like to give us feedback on our titles before they are published? Contact us at the address below – we'd love to hear from you!

Barrington Stoke, 10 Belford Terrace, Edinburgh EH4 3DQ
Tel: 0131 315 4933 Fax: 0131 315 4934
E-mail: info@barringtonstoke.co.uk
Website: www.barringtonstoke.co.uk

More Teen Titles!

Joe's Story by Rachel Anderson 1-902260-70-8
Playing Against the Odds by Bernard Ashley 1-902260-69-4
Harpies by David Belbin 1-842990-31-4
Firebug by Eric Brown 1-842991-03-5
TWOCKING by Eric Brown 1-842990-42-X
To Be a Millionaire by Yvonne Coppard 1-902260-58-9
All We Know of Heaven by Peter Crowther 1-842990-32-2
Ring of Truth by Alan Durant 1-842990-33-0
Falling Awake by Vivian French 1-902260-54-6
The Wedding Present by Adèle Geras 1-902260-77-5
The Cold Heart of Summer by Alan Gibbons 1-842990-80-2
Shadow on the Stairs by Ann Halam 1-902260-57-0
Alien Deeps by Douglas Hill 1-902260-55-4
Partners in Crime by Nigel Hinton 1-842991-02-7
Dade County's Big Summer by Lesley Howarth 1-842990-43-8
Runaway Teacher by Pete Johnson 1-902260-59-7
No Stone Unturned by Brian Keaney 1-842990-34-9
Wings by James Lovegrove 1-842990-11-X
A Kind of Magic by Catherine MacPhail 1-842990-10-1
Stalker by Anthony Masters 1-842990-81-0
Clone Zone by Jonathan Meres 1-842990-09-8
The Dogs by Mark Morris 1-902260-76-7
Turnaround by Alison Prince 1-842990-44-6
Dream On by Bali Rai 1-842990-45-4
All Change by Rosie Rushton 1-902260-75-9
Fall Out by Rosie Rushton 1-842990-74-8
The Blessed and The Damned by Sara Sheridan 1-842990-08-X
Double Vision by Norman Silver 1842991-00-0